When Mama
Comes Home Tonight

When Mama Comes Home Tonight

BY Eileen Spinelli

ILLUSTRATED BY Jane Dyer

Aladdin Paperbacks

New York London Toronto Sydney Singapore

Special thanks to Lynn and Willie
—J. D.

First Aladdin Paperbacks edition April 2002

Text copyright © 1998 by Eileen Spinelli
Illustrations copyright © 1998 by Jane Dyer

Aladdin Paperbacks
An imprint of Simon & Schuster
Children's Publishing Division
1230 Avenue of the Americas
New York, NY 10020

Designed by Paul Zakris. The text of this book was set in 30-point Venetian.
The illustrations were rendered on Waterford 140 lb. hot press paper with
Winsor & Newton watercolors and Caran D'Ache colored pencils.
Printed and bound in the United States of America
2 4 6 8 10 9 7 5 3 1

The Library of Congress has cataloged the hardcover edition as follows:
When Mama comes home tonight / written by Eileen Spinelli;
illustrated by Jane Dyer.
p.   cm.
Summary: When Mama arrives home, she and her child enjoy
a series of activities together before bedtime.
ISBN 0-689-81065-2 (hc.)
1. Mother and child—Fiction. 2. Bedtime—Fiction.
3. Stories in rhyme.
I. Dyer, Jane, ill.
PZ8.3.S759 Wh 1998
[E]—dc21
96-53141
ISBN 0-689-84897-8 (Aladdin pbk.)

To Joan McIntyre and the staff and
friends of Phoenixville Library
—E. S.

For all mothers who come home tired at the end
of the day—wishing you dances down the hall
—J. D.

When Mama comes home from work, dear child,
when Mama comes home tonight,
she'll cover you with kisses,
she'll hug you sweet and tight.

She'll feed you soup and applesauce,
she'll dance you down the hall,

she'll play a game of pat-a-cake,
she'll wrap you in her shawl.

She'll hold you at the window,

she'll help you count the cars.

She'll make three wishes in your name
and tell them to the stars.

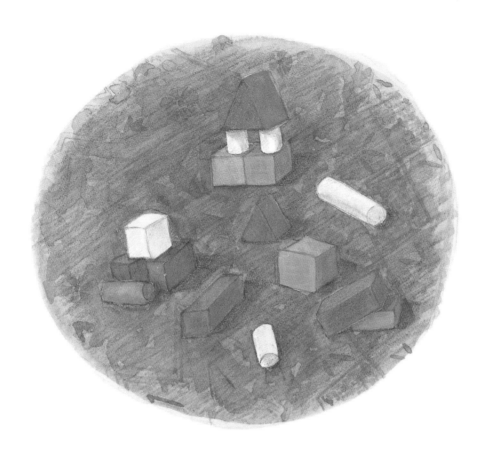

When Mama comes home from work, dear child,
when Mama comes home tonight,
she'll say, "Let's put your blocks away—
the red, the green, the white."

She'll fix herself a cup of tea
and let you have a sip.

She'll mend your blue pajamas

and her own pink satin slip.

She'll bathe you soft and gentle,
she'll brush your curly hair,

she'll read your favorite story
in the cozy rocking chair.

She'll find your tattered Teddy

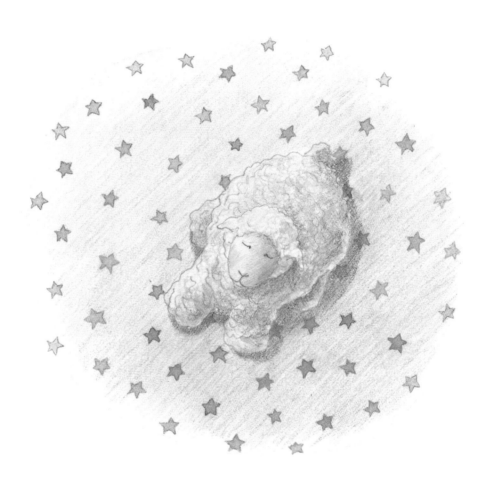

and your fuzzy little sheep.

She'll hush you down with lullabies
until you're near asleep.

She'll tuck you snug beneath the quilt
and leave on one small light,

when Mama comes home from work, dear child,
when Mama comes home tonight.